PAINT THE TOWN

By Crystal Velasquez   Illustrated by Jay Johnson

ISBN 0-439-83008-7
Copyright © 2006 Scholastic Entertainment Inc. All rights reserved.
SCHOLASTIC, MAYA & MIGUEL and logos are trademarks of Scholastic Inc.
12 11 10 9 8 7 6 5 4 3 2 1   6 7 8 9 10/0
Printed in the U.S.A.
First printing, November 2006

SCHOLASTIC INC.

New York   Toronto   London   Auckland   Sydney
Mexico City   New Delhi   Hong Kong   Buenos Aires

Maya, Miguel, and Maggie were drawing pictures at the community center one morning. Mrs. Temple, the director of the center, peeked at their work.

"Oh my!" she said. "You are so talented! If only I had your imagination. Maybe then I could add something exciting to this wall."

"*¡Eso es!*" Maya yelled, her ponytail bobbles
lighting up. "That's it!"

"Why don't we paint a giant mural?" Maya asked. "Miguel is a great artist and Maggie has a real eye for color. It's sure to be a success!"

Mrs. Temple clapped her hands and smiled. "That would be wonderful, Maya!"

"That sounds like fun," Maggie said. "What do you think, Miguel?"

"There's only one problem," he answered, biting his lip. "This wall is pretty big. We're going to need all the help we can get."

"Well, this is a community center," Mrs. Temple said. "Why don't we ask the community to help?"

"Miguel will have to give everyone a crash course in art, but the rest should be smooth sailing," Maya said confidently. "What could go wrong?"

But Miguel was worried. Maya's plans usually meant trouble!

Everyone in the neighborhood wanted to help.
Theo, Andy, and Chrissy volunteered right away.
Even Paco signed up!

Mrs. Temple had gathered all the art supplies they needed. Maggie brought clothes that people could model for the mural. And Miguel brought his sketchbook.

"Are you sure we can do this, Miguelito?"
Abuela asked.

"*¡Claro que sí!*" Miguel answered. "Of course
we can!" But he could tell that Abuela and her
friends weren't so sure.

"If you start with a subject you love, art can be easy—and fun!" Miguel said.

Paco flapped his wings and cleared his throat loudly. "Ah-HEM!"

Miguel laughed. "Okay, Paco. You will be my first subject!"

"And don't forget," Maggie added. "A little color—and the right outfit, of course—can make your picture even better!" She tied a bright green cape around Paco's neck.

Paco struck a superhero pose. **"SQUAAWK!**
I'm Super Paco!" Everyone giggled.

"That's great!" Theo said. "Andy and I have the perfect idea. A giant soccer match!"

"Does Paco get to paint?" the parrot asked. But Theo was too busy posing the bird as a soccer player.

"Not now, Paco. I'm inspired!" Theo answered.

"*Bwak*," Paco sulked.

"No, not soccer . . . it should be something more like this," Maggie said, pulling Paco toward her. She posed him with a feather boa and started painting a fashion show.

Everyone grabbed a brush and started painting. But they all had different ideas, which meant they kept Paco busy! "Paco, over here!" someone called, waving an Easter hat.

"*¡Paco, ayudamé!*" cried Tito, holding a pair of swimming goggles.

In all the excitement, the wall became very crowded. The pictures were starting to crash into one another!

"Oh no! Your soccer field is in our rain forest!" Abuela cried.

"And your fashion show is in the middle of our game," Theo said to Maggie. As he pointed with his paintbrush, he accidentally splattered yellow paint all over the picture.

When Maggie whipped around to answer Theo, a glob of red paint flew off her brush—right onto Andy's forehead.

"Oops!" she said, but it was too late.

Before Maya knew it, the mural project had turned into an all-out paint war!

"Miguel, this is getting out of control," Maya said. "We've got to do something!"

Miguel knew that look. "You have a plan, don't you?" he asked Maya.

Maya nodded. She stepped right into the middle of the crowd and yelled, "STOOOOOOOOP!"

"Look at what you're doing to the mural," Maya pointed out. Everyone looked guiltily at the ruined wall. "And look at what you've done to poor Paco!"

"*Sqwawk*," Paco muttered.

He looked so silly that they couldn't help but laugh.

Abuela laughed along with Rosa. "The kids are right. We've been so silly!"

"And Paco, I hope you can forgive us," Tito said, wiping off Paco's beak.

"Yeah," Maggie added. "Sorry, Paco. I guess we got carried away."

"But what should we really paint?" Andy asked.
Everyone stepped back to study the wall. When Maya saw how the art had blended together, she got a little inspiration of her own.

"*¡Tengo una idea!*" she cried. "I have an idea!"

"We can still use all of your ideas," Maya said, "but in a new way. What if you each pair up with someone who had a very different idea and try to work together?"

"That sounds great!" Theo raved. Everyone agreed and started pairing up.

With a little direction from Maya, the mural really came together. Maggie teamed up with Rosa to paint a fashion show starring the pet shop animals as runway models. And Abuela and her friends added themselves to Andy and Theo's soccer game!

But there was still something missing. Something to make it look like all the scenes were happening under one sky....

"The sun is missing," Maya declared. "We need a big, bright sun!"

"Paco?" she asked gently. "Will you do the honors?"
The parrot had never been so excited! He got right
to work.

Everyone cheered. "Great job, Paco!"

"Paco, you're a real artist now," Maggie said. "So you should wear this." Paco backed up nervously, but Maggie just put a simple artist's beret on his head.

"*Phew!*" Paco said in relief.

Mrs. Temple was delighted. "It's a masterpiece!" she declared.

Maya smiled. "Like I said, what could go wrong?"